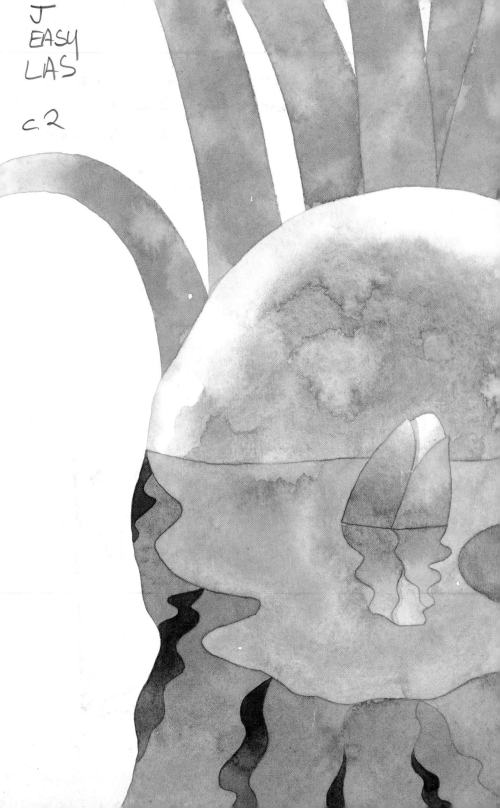

To Carole—wherever you are.

K.L.

For my mother

M.B.

Text copyright © 1995 by Kathryn Lasky
Illustrations copyright © 1995 by Mike Bostock

First U.S. edition 1995

Library of Congress Cataloging-in-Publication Data

Lasky, Kathryn.
Pond year / Kathryn Lasky ; illustrated by Mike Bostock.—1st U.S. ed.
Summary: Two young girls enjoy playing and exploring in the nearby
pond where they discover tadpoles, insects, wildflowers in the summer,
and a place to ice skate in the winter.
ISBN 1-56402-187-4 (reinforced trade ed.)
[1. Ponds—Fiction. 2. Nature—Fiction. 3. Play—Fiction.
4. Friendship—Fiction.]   I. Bostock, Mike, ill.   II. Title.
PZ7.L3274Po   1995
[E]—dc20   94-14834

10 9 8 7 6 5 4 3 2 1

Printed in Hong Kong

This book was typeset in Sabon.

The pictures in this book were done in watercolor.

Candlewick Press
2067 Massachusetts Avenue
Cambridge, Massachusetts 02140

POND YEAR

by Kathryn Lasky   illustrated by Mike Bostock

CANDLEWICK PRESS
CAMBRIDGE, MASSACHUSETTS

There's a pond out back
and down the hill from our
house. It's too shallow and
mucky to swim in. And in
August it smells like an old
wet mop. But my best friend
Carole and I like to play there
every day, all year round.

In April we gather twigs and
build little rafts. Sometimes
we stick leaves on for sails
and have races.

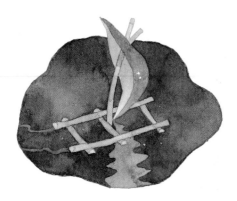

In May we start looking for frogs'
eggs. They float in clumps near
the surface like clear beads of jelly.
If you see the black dots you
know for sure that frogs
have started to grow.
We take our nets and
put the eggs in an
old punch bowl with
lots of pond water.

They grow a little bit and change shape.
In seven days you can see their
heads and tails. And in ten
days when the jelly
beads are very soft, the
first tadpoles squirm out.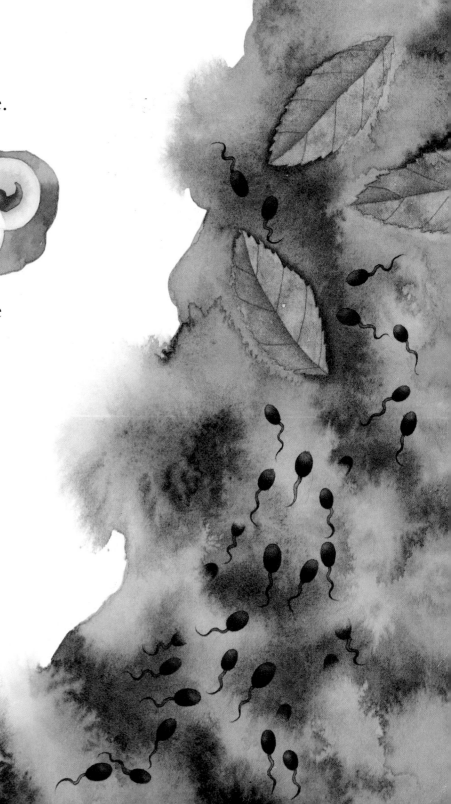

   We take the punch bowl down to the
pond and let them go. They swim to
rest near leaves or just under the fluffy
pond scum—algae that grows like
a green water carpet over the pond.

 Pond scum keeps
things warm and
wet and gives
creatures a safe
place to live.

In June when the water is
warmer, we might sneak a wade.
We don't call it wading, though.
We call it dipping. We dip in
our feet, and the water—all
silty with swirled-up mud—
leaves tan socks on them.
If we dip in up to our thighs,
it looks like silk stockings,
the kind our mothers wear
when they dress up.

When we get tired of putting on our mud silk, we just stand still, letting the oozy bottom goosh between our toes, and we look for our tadpoles. We spot one. Through its transparent skin you can see its front frog legs all folded up, almost ready to spring out.

Sometimes we dip around to the
darkest, muckiest corner of the pond
to look for its yellow secret on
the bank, where the woods begin.
The secret is lady's slippers, a
wildflower shaped like a lady's shoe.
It is a rare flower, my mom says.
It is so rare, she says it might
disappear and never
grow again.

By July one end of the pond is thick with algae and
buzzing with damselflies. And the tadpoles are finally frogs.
Their tails are gone, and they sit like little statues on rocks
or wait for flies underwater with their eyes bulging up
just above the surface.

Carole and I go looking for crawdaddies,
or crayfish. They have lots of legs, so they're
good at moving around.

We have contests to see
who can catch the most crawdaddies.
I once caught twenty-four in one morning.
We build a little mud slide for them and let them
have races on it. Then we put them
back in the pond.

We like mud
and we like scum.
We scoop the mud and
make mud cookies for
      our mud bakery.

We skim the scum
with our nets, and then
      we pick out the little bugs
      and set it out to dry.

One day we made
green wigs for all our old
bald-headed dolls.

Another time we twisted the dried
scum into thin strands and braided
friendship rings for each other and
promised to be best friends,
pond buddies, scum chums
forever.

By August the scum is so thick it clogs one end of the pond. At the other end are water lilies, and in between there is almost every kind of water bug you can think of: There are the dark gray water boatmen that paddle with their feet, and water striders that skim across the top and never break the surface. There are dragonflies and damselflies with transparent wings that flash in the sunlight. We collect all the dead bugs and look at them with our magnifying glasses. You can see the water boatmen's flat, stick-out feet and the scales of the dragonflies' wings. Up close, bug parts are amazing and special—just right for each bug.

In a sunny patch of water
near the bank, the salamanders
nestle in the ooze. There are
orange ones and dark brown
ones. We catch them
and let them crawl up
our legs in scrolly,
bright designs.
Then we wear
them when we
go dipping, and
they swim
right off.

In September the muskrats that live in holes on the banks get busy fixing their nests for winter. We have never seen a muskrat, but my father has. They are very shy. He says you have to come at night and be very patient. You cannot be wiggly little girls.

One night when the moon is full and the pond is like a silvery mirror, he takes us to wait for muskrats. We wear our pond buddy rings and swear to be quiet and patient. But it's hard. I hear the wind in the trees and I hear a bullfrog croak and I hear my breathing. I even hear my heart beating. Carole and I both start to wiggle. We wait and wait. It seems like an hour, but my dad whispers it's only been eight minutes.

Finally we give up. We've both got ten million itches, and little coughs scratching our throats. So I guess everybody on earth will have seen a muskrat except us. My dad says we will try again next year. Next year we'll be seven.

The days grow shorter and colder. The pond scum shrinks up until it is just a little patch in the corner. Early in the morning and again in the late afternoon, thin scarves of mist rise up from the still, black water of the pond.

The frogs and the salamanders grow slow and burrow into the quiet mud for a long winter's sleep.

The dragonflies and the damselflies have died long ago. Their eggs have hatched into nymphs, young insects without wings, that dig down under the rocks and sticks of the pond bottom.

By November the scum is gone. The pond is a black mirror. We can see our faces in its surface. We can see the color of our eyes in its blackness, count our teeth, and wiggle our noses without a ripple to wrinkle our reflections. We are so quiet and we are so still, but no muskrats come.

One morning in December there is ice, thin as a
dragonfly's wing. In January the ice is thick and we go
skating with my mom and dad and Carole's mom.
    I skate a loopy figure eight and think about the
salamanders frozen in their sleep, the groggy frogs all cozy
in the mud until spring, the dragonfly nymphs wingless
in the ooze without a thought of flight.

In February the ice begins to melt.

In March we make a tiny raft from twigs and count the days until frogs' eggs and lady's slippers, pond scum and mud silk.

And soon summer will come and the algae will grow thick. We start wishing our muskrat wishes. We promise never to go alone to wait for them. We will always go together and try to be quiet and try not to itch and try to be patient.

After all, we are pond buddies, scum chums—forever.